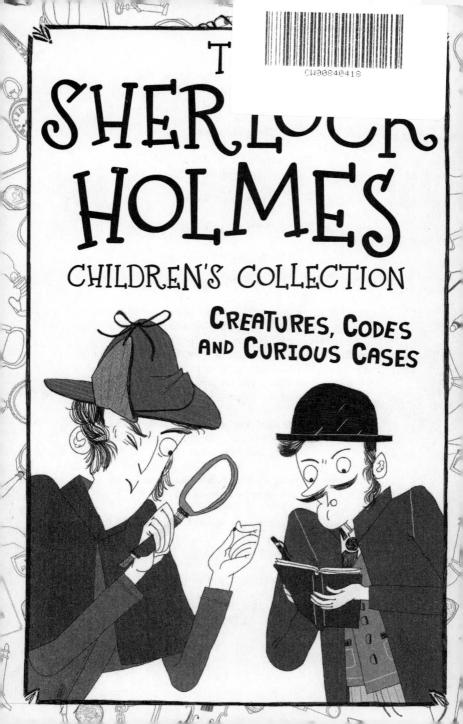

Published by Sweet Cherry Publishing Limited
Unit 36, Vulcan House,
Vulcan Road,
Leicester, LE5 3EF
United Kingdom

First published in the UK in 2021
2021 edition

2 4 6 8 10 9 7 5 3 1

ISBN: 978-1-78226-432-3

Cover design by Arianna Bellucci and Amy Booth
Illustrations by Arianna Bellucci

Lexile® code numerical measure L = Lexile® 720L

Guided Reading Level = W

www.sweetcherrypublishing.com

Printed and bound in India
I.TP002

SHERLOCK HOLMES

THE SOLITARY CYCLIST

SIR ARTHUR CONAN DOYLE

Chapter One

Holmes had been puzzling over an unsolved case all day. He had papers strewn all over his desk and was quiet except for the occasional muttering. I knew better than to talk – interrupting Holmes whilst he was working was never a wise idea. So I sat silently, reading my copy of

The Lancet to keep up with
medical news.

Our tea tray still lay on the
table, stacked with empty cups and
half-eaten biscuits. The floor was
carpeted with papers, scrapbooks
and beakers filled with
colourful chemicals.

I stood up to draw the blinds on the cloudy April evening. Suddenly there came a knock on the door of our sitting room. Holmes cursed and slapped the paper he was holding onto his desk.

It was our housekeeper, Mrs Hudson.

'Mrs Hudson! I am in the middle of some important work!' shouted Holmes.

Fortunately, Mrs Hudson was used to Holmes' outbursts and

her face stayed calm. 'There is a young lady here to see you,' she said. 'She said it was urgent.'

Holmes sighed. 'This is not a good time.'

'She is very persistent, Mr Holmes. She says she will not leave until she has seen you.'

Holmes nodded. 'All right. Show her up.'

'I would not disturb you if it were not very important,' said a voice from the doorway. The young

woman had been standing behind
Mrs Hudson the whole time.

She was tall and graceful. She
wore a plain brown dress that

was neat but far from new, and a small straw hat. She said that her name was Miss Violet Smith.

'Please, Mr Holmes,' she said. 'I need your help and advice urgently.'

I could see that Miss Smith was very anxious and determined to tell her story. Holmes must have realised it too.

'Please sit down,' Holmes said, with a weary smile. 'It must be urgent to bring you here at such a

late hour. The problem cannot be your health, however, because I can see that you are a keen cyclist.'

Miss Smith looked down at her feet and I followed her gaze. There was a slight scuffing on the inside of each shoe where they scraped against the pedals. She nodded, realising how Holmes had deduced this.

'Yes, I cycle a lot, Mr Holmes,' she said. 'And that has something to do with my visit to you today.'

'You live in the country,' said Holmes.

'Yes, sir. I live in Farnham now, on the border of Surrey. But, until recently, I lived in London, with my mother. My father is dead, Mr Holmes. His name was James Smith and he conducted the orchestra at the old Imperial Theatre. I am a musician too, but

I teach more than I play. When my father died, my mother and I were left without a relative in the world except for my uncle, Ralph Smith. He went to Africa twenty-five years ago, and we have not heard from him since.'

Holmes leaned forwards and pressed his fingertips together in the way he did when he was listening intently.

'We were left very poor,' Miss Smith continued, 'but one day, towards the end of last year, there was an advertisement in *The Times* asking of our whereabouts. I have it here.'

She opened the small bag she was carrying and handed a newspaper cutting to Holmes.

24ᵗʰ November 1894

PERSONAL

If anyone knows the whereabouts of Mrs Mary Smith and her daughter, Miss Violet Smith, sister-in-law and niece respectively, of Mr Ralph Smith, lately of South Africa, they should go to Carruthers & Co. solicitors, of 57 Welbeck Street, London.

'I presume you went?' asked Holmes.

'Yes. We were very excited. We thought my uncle may have died and left us a fortune in his will. We met two gentlemen there: Mr Carruthers, the lawyer, and Mr Woodley, who was visiting from South Africa. They said my uncle was a friend of theirs and had died some months before in Johannesburg. He had been very poor but had asked Mr Woodley to find us.'

'But if your uncle was poor, then surely he would not have had any money to leave you in his will. So why would he want to contact you after all this time?' asked Holmes.

'I do not know,' said Miss Smith. 'We thought it was strange too, as Uncle Ralph had taken no notice of us when he was alive. Mr Carruthers said that my uncle had heard about my father's death, and felt sorry that he had not kept in touch with us.'

'When was this meeting?' asked Holmes.

'Last December – four months ago.'

At that moment, Mrs Hudson came in with a fresh tray of tea. She stared in horror at the mess of the old tea tray and swiftly cleared it away, tutting as she left the room.

I poured out a cup for each of us. Miss Smith certainly needed a warm drink to calm her nerves. She sipped it politely while keeping her eyes fixed on Holmes.

'Please continue,' he said.

'Mr Woodley was a puffy-faced young man with a red moustache and beard,' said Miss Smith. 'He kept trying to flirt with me. I didn't like him at all. I was sure that Cyril wouldn't wish me to know such a person.'

'Ah, Cyril is his name!' said Holmes, smiling. He had guessed, as I had, that such a pleasant young woman must have a sweetheart.

Miss Smith blushed and laughed. 'Yes, Mr Holmes. Cyril Morton. He's an electrical engineer. We hope to get married at the end of summer.'

'I see. And what is Mr Carruthers like?'

'He is an older man and very nice. He has dark hair and no moustache.

He seemed quiet and polite. He asked about our finances, and when I told him that my mother and I were very poor, he offered me a job teaching music to his daughter, who is ten. He said I would be given a room in his house, Chiltern Grange, and he would pay me one hundred pounds a year. It was a very generous offer, but I explained that I didn't want to leave my mother.

When he said I could

go home every weekend to visit her,
I accepted the job at once. I packed
my bags that evening.'

'And did that work out well?'
Holmes asked.

Miss Smith nodded. 'Mr
Carruthers is a widower and lives
about six miles from Farnham.
His home, Chiltern Grange, is
large, yet has lots of windows on
every side, so it's wonderfully
light and welcoming inside. The
music room is very elegant and

Mr Carruthers' daughter, Sarah, is a joy to teach.

'Mr Carruthers is very musical too. We've spent many pleasant evenings together, talking about music and playing the piano. We both enjoy the same composers.'

'All would seem perfect then,' said Holmes as I poured us all another cup of tea.

Miss Smith's smile fell from her face. 'It was, until we had a visitor.'

'Mr Woodley,' said Holmes.

She looked surprised. 'However did you guess?'

'I never guess.' Holmes said with a wry smile.

'He came to stay for a week,' explained Miss Smith. 'He was a dreadful person and a bully to the staff. But to me he was worse. He boasted of his wealth and kept begging me to marry him. He promised me the finest diamonds in London, but I kept telling him I was not interested. I just wanted him to leave me alone. Once, when we were left alone for a moment, he tried to kiss me.' She shuddered at the memory.

'How awful!' I said.

'Luckily, Mr Carruthers came in at that moment and pulled him away from me,' Miss Smith explained. 'Then he punched Mr Woodley so hard that he fell and cut his face on the coffee table. It was horrible to watch, Mr Holmes. I had never seen such violence.

That was the end of his visit, of course. Mr Carruthers sent him home and apologised for his friend's behaviour.'

Both Holmes and I sank back into our chairs with a kind of relief. It seemed the villain was gone.

'But the real reason I have come to consult you, Mr Holmes, is because of a disappearing cyclist. Every Saturday morning I ride my bicycle to Farnham station to catch the twelve-twenty train into London to visit my mother for the weekend. The journey from Chiltern Grange to the station is a lonely one. To start with there are a few cottages, but after crossing the bridge over the little river, there is a sharp bend. After that is a long, straight road that is bordered by miles of open fields on one side and by the woods that surround Charlington Hall, a huge manor house, on the other. It's about a mile long, and it's rare to meet anyone at all along it.

'Two weeks ago I was cycling down that very road when I looked over my shoulder. About two hundred metres behind me was a man, also on a bicycle.

He seemed to be middle-aged and had a long black beard. By the time I got to Farnham Station he had gone, so I thought no more about it. But when I returned on Monday, there he was again.

And again on the next Saturday and the next Monday. If I slowed down, he did too, and if I stopped, he did too. It was the strangest thing, but, truly, I felt more curious than afraid.'

Holmes and I exchanged glances. This was certainly mysterious.

I could feel a thrill of excitement bubbling up within me.

Another adventure was beginning.

Chapter Two

'Did you tell Mr Carruthers about the cyclist?' asked Holmes.

'Yes, I did. He said he would order a horse and dog-cart to

Dog-cart

A simple wooden cart drawn by one horse and used on country estates. Some have a bench for the driver and one passenger, others have back-to-back seats. They have a tendency to throw mud onto the left side. Originally the rear seat folded down to make room for dogs, hence the name.

take me to and from the station in future. But it failed to arrive this weekend, so I cycled again. And the same man appeared this morning, as usual.'

'Can you describe him more fully, Miss Smith?'

'I couldn't see his face clearly because he kept his distance and wore a cloth cap, but I was sure it wasn't someone I knew. He was dressed in a dark suit and all I could see of his face was the black beard.

'This morning I was determined to find out what he wanted. I stopped cycling and he stopped too. Then I pedalled very quickly around a bend in the road and stopped to wait for him. I expected him to shoot round after me, but he never appeared. I only wanted to ask him why he was following me.

'I went back and looked around the corner. I could see a full mile of road, but he wasn't there.

And there is no side road, Mr Holmes. There was nowhere for him to escape. He simply disappeared.'

Holmes chuckled and rubbed his hands. 'This is certainly a strange

case. How long was it from when you turned the corner to when you went back and saw the empty road?'

'Two or three minutes,' said Miss Smith.

'Then he couldn't have taken a path over the fields, or you would have seen him. He must have gone up the drive to Charlington Hall.'

Miss Smith sighed and nodded. 'I just *had* to come and see you, Mr Holmes. I was sure you would be able to solve the puzzle.'

'Where does your fiancé live?'
asked Holmes.

'He lives in Coventry. He
works for the Midland Electrical
Company there.'

'There's no chance he would
pay you a surprise visit?'

'Oh, Mr Holmes, I think I
would recognise him! Even from
two hundred metres away.'

'Do you have any other
admirers who may be following
you?' I asked.

'No. Only that dreadful man, Mr Woodley. Yet it does sometimes seem that my employer, Mr Carruthers, takes an extra interest in me, although he has never said anything. He is a perfect gentleman, but a girl always knows.'

'Ha!' said Holmes. 'What does he do for a living?'

'He goes to London once or twice a week, to buy and sell shares in South African gold mines. He is a rich man.'

Holmes stood up. 'I see. Please let me know if anything new happens, Miss Smith. I am very busy now, but I will make some enquiries. Don't do anything without letting me know. Goodbye.'

Miss Smith looked a little surprised at Holmes' sudden curtness. She stood, thanked us both, and shook our hands before leaving.

'It wouldn't be unusual for such an attractive young lady to have admirers, as you suggested, Watson,' Holmes said. 'But it would be strange for them to

repeatedly follow her on a bicycle along a lonely country road.' He lit his pipe and leaned back in his chair.

I knew he

was getting ready to mull over all the facts in his mind. 'There are some strange things about this case, Watson.'

'It's odd that he only appears on that same stretch of road each time,' I said.

'It is odd indeed. First, we shall find out who lives at Charlington Hall and then we shall uncover the connection between Mr Carruthers and Mr Woodley. Such very different men. Why should they *both* be trying to find Ralph Smith's relations? Odd, Watson ... very odd!'

'Are you going to go to Farnham then?' I asked.

'No, my dear fellow. *You* are.'

Chapter Three

I looked at Holmes in surprise.
'Me?'

'I don't want to interrupt my important research for what might prove to be a trivial matter,' Holmes said. 'It could be that this man simply cycles the same route as Miss Smith on the same days she does. No, no, I'm quite sure it should be you. On Monday morning you will go to Farnham and hide somewhere along that lonely stretch of road Miss Smith described. Then you can see for yourself what happens when she cycles back from the station. After that, find out who lives at Charlington Hall and then come back here and report to me.'

We knew that Miss Smith usually caught the nine-fifty train

from Waterloo to Farnham on Monday mornings, so I went early and caught the eight-thirteen train. That way, I knew I would have time to hide near Charlington Hall before she arrived.

The road was just as she said: long and straight with the open grassy fields on one side and the woods surrounding Charlington Hall on the other. The main gates of Charlington Hall sat just before the woods. They were covered from top to bottom in thick tendrils of ivy and opened onto a long driveway. Although I could only see snippets of the hall itself through the trees,

it was clear that the building was neglected and decaying. There was certainly something creepy about the place.

The fields, on the other hand, were golden with buttercup flowers that gleamed in the bright spring sunshine. I hid behind a bush nearby so that I could see every angle of the road and the driveway leading to Charlington Hall.

Then, as I watched, a cyclist appeared. He was coming in

the opposite direction from Farnham Station. He was dressed in a dark suit and had a black beard, exactly as Miss Smith had described. When he reached the driveway of Charlington Hall, he jumped off his bicycle and disappeared behind the hedge.

Clearly this was no coincidence. This was not someone who happened to be travelling the same way as Miss

Smith. He was deliberately waiting to follow her.

After fifteen minutes, another cyclist appeared. This time

it was Miss Smith coming from the station. She looked about her as she reached the Charlington Hall driveway. As soon as she had passed, the man came out, got on his bicycle, and followed her.

In the whole landscape those were the only moving figures, the graceful girl sitting up straight on her bicycle and the man bent low over his handlebars.

Miss Smith looked back and slowed down. He slowed down too. She stopped. He stopped. Suddenly, she whisked her bicycle around and dashed straight at him. She rode at an incredible speed, but he was just as quick.

He turned and sped off into the distance. After a while, Miss Smith gave up and turned around to continue on her route. But the man suddenly appeared again. He was *still* following her. He was certainly persistent. They both

disappeared around a bend in the road.

I waited in my hiding place for a moment, and it's just as well I did. After a few minutes, the man came back round the corner and cycled straight through the open gates of Charlington Hall, and up

the driveway. I ran across the road and a little way up the drive until I could see the old grey building with its cluster of chimneys, but the man was nowhere to be seen. Perhaps he worked there, as a butler or a chef? He wasn't dressed like a gardener, and there wasn't much evidence of anyone caring for the garden. He couldn't possibly be the master of the house, could he?

Then I remembered what Holmes had said about finding

out who owned the place. I walked
to Farnham town and asked in an
estate agent's about the owner of
the hall. They said it had just been
rented for the summer to a Mr
Williamson – a respectable elderly
gentleman. That was all the agent
could tell me.

When I got back to Baker
Street, Holmes listened carefully
to my long report but didn't
give any praise at the end of
it. I thought I had done a good

job, but his face showed just the opposite.

'Your hiding place, my dear Watson, was wrong. You should have been nearer Charlington Hall. Then you would have got a closer view of the man. Even Miss Smith was closer than you. You really have done rather badly. And you went to an estate agent to find out about the house?'

'Where else should I have gone?' I said, a little crossly.

'To the nearest pub, of course. That is the centre of country gossip. They would have told you the name of everyone from the master to the scullery maid.

'Mr Williamson, you say. Well, if he is an elderly man, then it isn't him speeding along on a bicycle. What have we gained by your expedition? It proves that Miss Smith's story is true – I never doubted it was. It confirms, too, that there is a connection between

the cyclist and Charlington Hall.
Yet we knew that as well. Oh,
Watson, don't look so upset. We
can do no more until Saturday,
but in the meantime I shall make
a few enquiries myself.'

The next morning we had a
note from Miss Smith.

Chiltern Grange   May 1895

Dear Mr Holmes,
It has happened again. The strange bearded
man on the bicycle followed me, as usual, this
morning. I tried suddenly turning and racing
towards the man, but he was just as quick.

Things have become very difficult for me at Chiltern Grange. Mr Carruthers has asked me to marry him. I am sure he loves me, but I am, as you know, engaged to someone else. I could see that he was very disappointed when I refused. I feel I must leave here immediately. It is such a shame. I have never been so well paid in my life, and my mother and I need the money. I shall miss my student, Sarah, very much, too.

Yours,
Violet Smith

'This case seems to be more interesting than I thought,' said Holmes, putting the letter down on the table. 'I think a quiet day in the country would do me good. I'll go to Farnham this afternoon and test one or two ideas I have.'

But the day wasn't as quiet as Holmes had hoped. Late that evening he arrived back in Baker Street with a cut lip and a bruised lump on his forehead.

'Holmes!' I cried. 'What happened?'

He laughed heartily, then grimaced when his lip hurt. 'It's always a treat to get some exercise. You know that I've had some experience of boxing, Watson? Well, today it came in useful.'

'Whatever happened?' I asked. 'It looks as though you lost the fight.'

'Not at all. I won by miles' he said.

'Tell me what happened,' I said.

'I found the country pub
that I'd suggested to you, and a
very talkative landlord gave me
some information. Williamson
is a white-bearded man and he
lives alone with a small staff.
There is a rumour that he was
once a church minister but did
something terrible and was
dismissed. The landlord said
there were usually weekend
visitors at Charlington Hall,

whom he called "a loud lot",
especially one with a red beard
called Mr Woodley.'

'Ha!' I said. 'So he didn't leave
Farnham when Mr Carruthers
threw him out.'

'We were just talking about
him when he walked in,' Holmes
continued. 'He had been in
the next room and had heard
everything. He was furious. He
asked who I was and why I was
asking questions. He finished

by swearing at me and swiping me across the face with the back of his hand. As you can see, he didn't miss. But the next few minutes were delicious! My reactions were as quick as a cat, and he was the one that went home in a dog-cart, holding a wet cloth to his head.

'I've come home with a few bruises, but I did learn a lot.'

I tutted at Holmes. Only he could manage to turn a quiet pub into a boxing ring. Nevertheless, I couldn't help worrying about him, and got out my medical bag to tend his wounds. I managed to get some ointment on his bruises before he impatiently waved me away and gave me one of his glares so that I didn't argue.

Chapter Four

On Thursday we received another note from Miss Smith.

Chiltern Grange   May 1895

Dear Mr Holmes,

I am definitely leaving my job. Even the high pay cannot make me stay. That horrible man, Mr Woodley, has come back. I saw him through the window talking to Mr Carruthers. He looked more frightening than ever. He seems to have

had an accident — his face is covered with cuts
and bruises.

Later I saw him skulking in the bushes. I
would rather have a wild animal loose around
the grounds than have him stalking about.

I shall be leaving on Saturday. Mr Carruthers
now has a dog-cart I can travel to the station
in, so the dangers of the lonely bit of road
are over.

Thank you for any work you have done
on my behalf, but I shall no longer need your
services.

Yours,

Violet Smith

I was relieved to hear the news, but Holmes said, 'There is something strange going on, Watson. It is our duty to see that nothing happens to Miss Smith on that last journey. We must both go to Farnham on Saturday morning and make sure that this strange affair has a happy ending.'

I had not really thought of the case as being dangerous. It seemed to me just strange.

It was certainly unpleasant for Miss Smith to be followed, but the man had never come closer than two hundred metres to her. The only dangerous part was Mr Woodley. He had tried to forcibly kiss her once, which is a vile, horrid thing to do, but he had never attacked her again. And I did not think Mr Woodley was the mysterious man on the bicycle – his beard was red, not black. Nevertheless, if Holmes thought it was important to watch over Miss Smith, then I was only too pleased to help.

Saturday was a sunny day after a night of rain. The glowing clumps of wild flowers looked beautiful to Holmes and I as we walked along the wide road towards Charlington Hall. Even Holmes, who often did not notice such beauty, commented on it.

'Well. This is a nice change from the drab, slate-grey of London, Watson,' he said.

'Indeed,' I agreed. 'It feels as if nothing dangerous could happen in such a pretty place.'

'Ah, Watson. As I've told you before, being in the countryside does not protect you from crime. Anything could happen out–'

His thoughts were interrupted by the appearance of a dog-cart. It was so far away across the hills, it looked like a black dot on the scenery. But it was moving very quickly towards us.

Holmes slapped his hand to his forehead. 'If that is Mr Carruthers' dog-cart, then Miss Smith must be going for an earlier train,' he said. 'We won't be at Charlington Hall in time to spot the mysterious cyclist!'

Holmes began running along the road. I could hardly keep up. After a few minutes, we lost sight of the dog-cart. Then, suddenly, Holmes stopped and threw his hands in the air.

The dog-cart had appeared again on the road in front of us, the horse

running wild. It was empty. There was not even a driver aboard.

'Too late, Watson! Too late!' cried Holmes. 'Why didn't I allow for an earlier train? It could be kidnap! Or murder! Block the road! Stop the horse!'

I walked out in front of the frightened horse and grabbed at the reins. Holmes and I brought the cart to a stop, turned it around and then jumped aboard. Holmes gave a flick of the reins

and we flew along the road
towards Charlington Hall.

'There's our man!' I cried.

A solitary cyclist was coming
towards us. His head was down
and his shoulders were hunched
as he put all his effort into
pushing the pedals.

Suddenly, he raised his
bearded face and saw us. He
stopped and sprung from the
bicycle. His face was pale and his
eyes were bright and angry.

'Stop!' he shouted. 'Stop! Where did you get that dog-cart?' He turned his bicycle to block our way.

Holmes sprang from the cart. 'You're the man we want to see. Where is Miss Violet Smith?'

'That's what I am asking you! You're in her dog-cart. You should know where she is.'

'We saw the dog-cart on the road. There was no one in it,' said Holmes. 'We drove back to help the young lady.'

'Good Lord! What shall I do?' cried the stranger in despair. 'They've got her, that scoundrel, Woodley, and the church minister. Come, man, come, if you really are her friend! We must save her, even if it costs me my life!'

He ran towards a gap in the hedge. Holmes followed him. I jumped down from the dog-cart and left the horse grazing at the side of the road before following too.

'This is where they came through,' said Holmes, pointing to some footprints on the muddy path. 'Wait, stop a minute. Who's this in the bushes?'

A young fellow of about seventeen lay on his back with his knees drawn up. He was alive but unconscious. He had a cut on his forehead, but I could see that it was not too deep.

'That's Peter, the horse groom,' cried the stranger. 'He was

driving the dog-cart with Miss
Smith in. The beasts have hit him
on the head. Leave him for now.
We cannot do anything for him,
but we must save Miss Smith
from a worse fate.'

My instincts told me to stop and
tend to the groom, but Holmes
pulled me onwards. I followed him
and the black-bearded stranger as
we ran frantically down the path,
through the woods and towards
Charlington Hall.

'They didn't go into the house,' said Holmes, stopping. 'Here are their footprints near this bush.'

As he spoke, we heard a woman's shrill scream. It vibrated through the woodland and ended suddenly

with a sort of choking gurgle.

'This way!' shouted the stranger.

We broke through into a clearing in the trees. On the far side, under a mighty oak, there stood a group of three people.

One was Miss Smith. She was drooping as if she were about to faint and had a handkerchief tied around her mouth so she couldn't speak. Opposite her was a brutal, heavy-faced man with a red moustache. I knew almost

immediately that this must be Mr
Woodley. He stood with a smug
smile on his face, waving a horse

whip in the air as if he'd just won a race. Between Miss Smith and Mr Woodley stood an elderly, grey-bearded man wearing the clothes of a church minister. He was putting a prayer book into his pocket as we arrived, and slapping Mr Woodley on the back as if to congratulate him.

'They're married!' I gasped.

'Come on!' cried the stranger. He rushed across the clearing with Holmes behind him.

Mr Williamson, the ex-minister, bowed at us with mock politeness. 'Let me introduce you to Mrs Woodley,' he said, pointing to Miss Smith as she staggered against a tree.

Mr Woodley marched towards us, chuckling. 'You  can take your beard off, Bob,' he said.

The stranger beside us snatched

84

off his fake black beard and flung it to the ground. Then he pulled out a gun and pointed it at Mr Woodley. 'Yes, it is I, Mr Carruthers. And I'll save this woman if it costs me my life.'

'You're too late!' shouted Mr Woodley. 'She's my wife now!'

'No,' cried Mr Carruthers. 'She's your widow!' And he fired his gun.

Chapter Five

As the gunshot sounded, Mr Woodley fell to the ground. Blood streamed from his chest.

Mr Williamson, the minister, pulled out a gun of his own, but Holmes was too quick for him. Like lightning, he lunged forwards and swiped the weapon out of the old man's hand.

'Enough of this!' Holmes said,
coldly. He put the gun in his pocket,
and warned Mr Williamson not
to move. 'Drop your gun too, Mr
Carruthers. We'll have no more
violence. Hand it over!'

'Who are you?' asked Mr
Carruthers, as if he had just
remembered we were there.

'My name is Sherlock Holmes.'

'Good heavens!'

'I see you have heard of me. I
will take charge until the police

arrive.' He looked around and then shouted to the frightened horse groom who had appeared through the trees, holding a handkerchief to the cut on his head. 'Here, lad, take this note and ride as fast as you can to Farnham Police Station.'

Holmes scribbled a few words on a page from his notebook.

Dear Superintendent,

Please send some police officers to the grounds of Charlington Hall, quickly. A young woman has been kidnapped and forced to marry. I have confiscated all weapons, but one man has been shot and needs to go to hospital. I have placed the other two men under arrest until the proper authority arrives.
I am a friend and colleague of Inspector Lestrade of Scotland Yard.

Yours,
Sherlock Holmes

The groom took the note and
ran to the horse we had left
grazing at the edge of the woods.

Then, under the glare of Holmes,
Mr Williamson and Mr Carruthers
carried Mr Woodley into the house
and laid him on a bed. I helped
the frightened woman into a chair
and gently untied the handkerchief
from around her mouth, being
careful not to hurt her further.

Then I examined Mr Woodley.
'He will live,' I said.

'What!' cried Mr Carruthers, springing from his chair. 'Don't tell me that this angel is to be tied to him for life!'

'You don't need to worry about that,' said Holmes, sitting down at a desk in the corner of the room. 'Mr Williamson has no right to marry people. He is no longer a minister, because he was dismissed in disgrace.'

'Once a minister, always a minister,' growled Mr Williamson.

'No,' said Holmes. 'That is not true. In any case, a forced marriage like this is not legal. It is a serious crime. You'll have time to think about it and regret your actions over the next ten years or so in prison. As to you, Mr Carruthers, you should have kept your gun in your pocket.'

'I think you are right, Mr Holmes, but I had to protect this woman,' said Mr Carruthers. 'I love her very much, and couldn't bear to think that she was in the power of this brute. I have never once let her go past this house alone, knowing that these rascals were lurking inside. I followed her on my bicycle to make sure she came to no harm.'

'Why didn't you tell her of the danger?' asked Holmes.

'Because she would have given up her job! I couldn't bear that. Even if she didn't love me, it was enough to have her around the house and to hear her voice.'

'You call that love, Mr Carruthers, but I would call it selfishness,' said Holmes.

'Maybe it is,' said Mr Carruthers, 'but she needed someone to look after her when the telegram came.'

Holmes looked at him sharply.

'What telegram?'

Mr Carruthers took a telegram from his pocket and showed it to us.

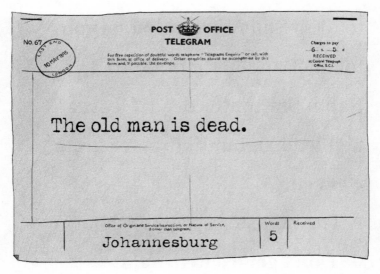

That was all it said.

Chapter Six

'Ah,' said Holmes. 'So you all lied
to Miss Smith before, when you
told her and her mother that
Ralph Smith was dead. He was
not dead, not until that telegram
was sent.'

The minister began to shout.

'Don't get excited,' said
Holmes, calmly leaning back

in his chair. 'The case is clear enough against you. I do, however, have a few questions to satisfy my curiosity. I know that the three of you came from South Africa together with an evil plot in mind. You, Mr Williamson, and Mr Carruthers and Mr Woodley.'

'Ha! You are incorrect,' said Mr Williamson, falling right into Holmes' trap. 'I never saw either of them until two months ago and I have never been in Africa in my life, Mr Busybody Holmes!'

'What he says is true,' said Mr Carruthers.

Holmes smiled. 'Well then. Two of you came over from South Africa. You had both known Ralph Smith and knew that he wouldn't live long. You found out that his niece, Miss Smith, would inherit his fortune. Is that right so far?'

Mr Carruthers nodded. Miss Smith gasped, but was too tired and shaken to say anything.

'So the two of you came to England to look for the girl,' said Holmes. 'The idea was that one of you was to marry her and the other would have a share of the inheritance money. For some reason, Mr Woodley was chosen to be the husband. Why was that?'

'We played cards for her on the voyage over,' said Mr Carruthers, hanging his head in shame.

I looked at him with horror.
Miss Violet Smith was the prize
in a card game! How could people
be so greedy for money that they
could use another person like this?

Holmes' face was blank, but I
knew that he shared my disgust.

'So you employed her to
teach your daughter music, Mr
Carruthers. Then Mr Woodley
came to make friends with her,
but she saw what a brute he was.

100

To complicate things, you fell in love with her yourself. And you couldn't bear the thought of Mr Woodley marrying her.'

'No, I couldn't!' cried Mr Carruthers.

Holmes nodded. 'You had a quarrel and Mr Woodley left in a rage to make his own plans.'

Mr Carruthers looked at Mr Williamson. 'It seems to me that this gentleman knows it all,' Mr Carruthers said with a bitter laugh. 'I found out that Mr Woodley had met this minister and they were living here in Charlington Hall, on the road Miss Smith had to pass to get to the train station each weekend. I kept my eye on her after that, because I knew they were up to something.

'Two days ago, Mr Woodley came to my house with this telegram saying that Ralph Smith was dead. He asked if I would stand by our agreement and convince her to marry him. I said I would not. He asked if I would marry Miss Smith myself and give him his share. I said that she did not want to marry me.'

'And what did Mr Woodley say?' asked Holmes.

'He said that it did not matter whether she *wanted* to marry me, as we could force her to marry. I said I would have nothing to do with such violence.

'Miss Smith said she was leaving the job and my home at the weekend. I had ordered a dog-cart to take her to the station, but I also followed on my bicycle. I couldn't keep up with the cart though, and after only a few minutes I saw you two gentlemen appear in it.'

Holmes stood up. 'I have heard enough. Now, I see three policemen coming up the drive and Peter, the horse groom, seems none the worse for his bang on the head. Can you look after Miss Smith, Watson? If she has recovered enough, we shall take her to her mother's house. We shall send for your fiancé, Miss Smith. I hope that will help you feel a little better.

'As for you, Mr Carruthers,

you have done some unforgivable
things. However, I think you did
what you could to stop the evil
plot you were a part of. Here is
my card. I would be happy to give
evidence for you in your trial.'

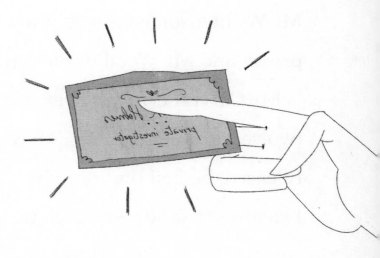

Chapter Seven

Mr Williamson and Mr Woodley
went to trial and were found
guilty of kidnapping and assault.
Mr Williamson got seven years in
prison and Mr Woodley got ten.

Mr Carruthers was given just
two years in prison. After he was
released, he fled the country.
I suspect that he went back to

South Africa, but we shall never know for sure.

As for Miss Violet Smith, she did inherit a large fortune from her uncle. And she married Mr Cyril Morton at the end of summer, as planned. I felt privileged to be invited to the wedding, and Holmes

tried to enjoy it, although I knew that he was not fond of parties. The fact that he went at all showed how much he cared for Miss Smith.

Her husband, Cyril Morton, became a senior partner in an electrical company in London. He and Miss Smith live a wonderfully happy life together. She even writes to us from time to time, telling us about their latest adventures.

Sherlock Holmes

World-renowned private detective Sherlock Holmes has solved hundreds of mysteries, and is the author of such fascinating monographs as *Early English Charters* and *The Influence of a Trade Upon the Form of a Hand.* He keeps bees in his free time.

Dr John Watson

Wounded in action at Maiwand, Dr John Watson left the army and moved into 221B Baker Street. There he was surprised to learn that his new friend, Sherlock Holmes, faced daily peril solving crimes, and began documenting his investigations. Dr Watson also runs a doctor's practice.

To download Sherlock Holmes activities, please visit www.sweetcherrypublishing.com/resources